UNO, DOS, TRES: ONE, TWO, THREE

by PAT MORA
Illustrated by BARBARA LAVALLEE

CLARION BOOKS/New York

Clarion Books
a Houghton Mifflin Company imprint
215 Park Avenue South, New York, NY 10003

The illustrations for this book were executed in watercolors on 300-lb. Fabriano watercolor board.
The text was set in 22/25-point Goudy.

Printed in Singapore

Library of Congress Cataloging-in-Publication Data

Mora, Pat.
Uno, dos, tres : One, two, three / by Pat Mora ; illustrated by Barbara Lavallee.
p.   cm.
Summary: Pictures depict two sisters going from shop to shop buying birthday presents for their mother.
Rhyming text presents numbers from one to ten in English and Spanish.
ISBN 0-395-67294-5   PA ISBN 0-618-05468-5
[1. Birthdays—Fiction. 2. Counting. 3. Stories in rhyme. 4. Spanish language materials]
I. Lavallee, Barbara, ill.   II. Title   III. Title: One, two, three.
PZ8.3.M794Un   1996
[E]—dc20   94-15337
CIP
AC

TWP 20 19 18 17 16 15 14 13 12

For my daughters, Libby and Cissy,
who give me so many wonderful surprises
—P.M.

To Marilyn—
with peaches, prunes, and happy times
—B.L.

uno   one

We'll buy Mamá a sun.

dos   two

Two doves that say coo-coo.

12   tres   three

Bells ring-ringing in our tree.

14   uno   dos   tres

one two three

cuatro   four

Piñatas at the door.

cinco   five

Puppets dance as if alive.

seis   six

Castanet click-clicks.

21

uno   dos   tres

one two three

cuatro   cinco   seis

four   five   six

uno   dos   tres
cuatro   cinco   seis

26

one   two   three
four   five   six

siete   seven

Stars twink-twinkling in heaven.

ocho eight

Small baskets, pots, and plates.

nueve   nine

Wood animals are fine.

diez   ten

A band of marching men.

36   uno   dos   tres   one   two   three

cuatro cinco seis   four five six   37

uno   dos   tres
cuatro cinco   seis

one   two   three
four   five   six

uno   dos   tres   cuatro   cinco
seis   siete   ocho   nueve   diez

one two three four five
six seven eight nine ten

41

¡Feliz cumpleaños, Mamá!

Happy birthday, Mama!

Author's Note

Since I grew up on the border, I started enjoying Mexican markets when I was a little girl. I've always liked the life in the markets—the music, the voices of the vendors, the splashes of color, the varied textures of the wares, the humor and inventiveness of folk artists, the sounds of Spanish and English weaving through the air.

Markets are wonderful places to buy surprises for those we love of all ages. We count our gifts in English, in Spanish—one, two, three . . . uno, dos, tres—enjoying the pleasure of being bilingual.

Pronunciation Guide

uno (OO-noh): one
dos (dohs): two
tres (trehs): three
cuatro (KWAH-troh): four
cinco (SEEN-koh): five
seis (SEH-ees): six
siete (SEE-eh-teh): seven
ocho (OH-choh): eight
nueve (NWEH-beh): nine
diez (dee-EHS): ten
Mamá (mah-MAH): Mama
piñata (pee-NYAH-tah): piñata
¡Feliz cumpleaños! (feh-LEES koom-pleh-AH-nyohs): Happy birthday!